The Low End

By

Author Larry Earl Toombs

Contents

I would like to dedicate this book to my mother

Jannie Mae (Sims) Toombs

Cp.1 Crimes, abductees

It was a hot normal day in Philadelphia in the suburbs called the low end. There were many houses and people of all nationalities who lived there and the residents got along very well with each other.

The rich people who lived in the luxury downtown area in Philadelphia had fine luxury houses and five star hotels many people of status wouldn't go to those hard living conditions because either they thought they were too much or they just didn't want to deal or associate with anyone in Philadelphia.

The only time you saw a predominately white or black figure was when they were coming to pick up their workers and drop them off when the workers was finishing working for their contractors.

These suburbs was called the Low End because of some of the low things that they did like being involved in high crimes or the way the area looked however these was real people living in the low end who lived a regular life on the daily bases.

Since the police wouldn't normally patrol in the low end unless something happened. It was a community that simple governed itself from the morning until the evening. You could get anything you wanted in the Low End. Many people who had warrants or even thugs who had high crimes would often hide in there.

The people in this community loved each other very seldom an argument broke out with the residents there unless someone owed drug money or somebody broke into someone house and stole something.

It was a very hot day when Jose’ decided to break and enter into a resident home and steal food out of the refrigerator. Jose’ had gotten away with it until he was heard gossiping on the streets about how he broke into the home and stole everything. The people who he stole the food from heard the word that it was in fact Jose. He broke into Maria house who happened to be Hispanic but Maria nephew was a nice guy to everyone but he did not play about his family.

The next day in the low end on a hot summer’s day Ramirez confronted Jose about breaking into his auntie house and stealing all her food. Ramirez also told him that his little cousin was an infant baby and she was sleeping in the next room of the house he broke and entered into and stole food also other items.

He also warned Jose's that if he break into his auntie house again something bad would happen to him but before Ramirez could get his last word out Jose' who was known for carrying a gun immediately pulled a nine millimeter out on him.

Ramirez told Jose that if he didn't pull the

trigger he would be back to get him. Well they were all friends living in the suburbs, they may argue with each other but they didn't want to kill each other so he didn't pull the trigger. He let Ramirez go free which turned out to be his worst mistake.

The gun was place to his head but he was allowed to walk away so he regrouped and told his friends that Jose' broke into his aunt house and stole food while her infant baby was sleeping in the next room. He also explained that he loved his baby cousin Alexia very much and he would kill someone over his little baby infant cousin. Once this information was told to his friends they immediately grabbed their artillery. Everyone waited two days hoping Jose would forget and just as they planned he forgot all about what he had done and thought everything was ok.

Two days later Ramirez sent a teenage boy around the corner to see where exactly Jose's location was. The teenager was unseen and undetected. He reported Ramirez the news of the suspect they were looking for was on the 3rd street with his shirt off drinking on a forty ounce of beer and talking to girls. He had completely forgotten about the robbery and the food he stole from the house just day's ago. Once the report was given to the men on Jose's whereabouts, the men suited up and surprised him.

All you could hear was skid marks from the tires screeching from the tires of an angry fed up mob of people who was ready in full gear to retaliate. Jose' was completely caught off guard and slightly drunk after a few shots were fired at him from a white old school Impala with hydraulics on it but they were all warning shots, they weren't trying to kill him but teach him a lesson.

The next day after surviving the drive by the victim sent a message that he was sorry for breaking into the family house stealing food also he was sorry he entered the house while the infant baby was sleeping in the next room but his pleads to squash the beef fell upon deaf ears.

The driver who was driving the white impala sent a word back to him that said, "I was trying to hit you."

The driver of the white old school Chevy was African American and he could speak Spanish too. He agreed to squash the beef with Jose' if he returned all the food he stole from the house he entered.

He agreed to do so but no one could speak Spanish fluently so they had Maria to write down a list of things in English the thief stole because Maria spoke English and Spanish. Once Maria wrote down the list it included bacon, eggs, juice, sugar, beer, some personal items etc. The driver of the white Chevy was nothing to play with and he warned Jose' that if every single item was not returned it would be the last time that people ever saw him or heard from him again.

All of the food items were returned the very next day and the beef with Jose' was squashed. He was warned to stay away from the house and to especially stay away from the infant baby who was sleeping in the house that he broke and entered into.

Everything was agreed to by the food thief

and he was allowed to go on with his life as if nothing had happened if he promised to never go near Maria house again. Seemingly everything returned to normal in the Low End and everything was back to business as normal.

If you mind your business and keep your nose clean nothing would happen to you in the hood because even if you were innocent and a bully picked on you the community would step in and help fight your battles for you. Night fell on the small poor town and a resident was frantically screaming down the street yelling,

"My daughter has not returned home and she was last seen with a guy in a black van that was speeding real fast." She called the police to the crime normally the police were afraid to come to the Low End but this was an emergency.

The police that was placed on this assignment was called Big Bo and he was known to get his man and bring him in to justice. The first thing Big Bo the policeman did was watch the evening news.

While watching the evening news he saw a conspiracy going on in Minnesota, a string of girls was coming up missing and he thought that they might have been hiding in the projects since it was a place for fugitives to hide and no one would ever suspect a kidnapper or a murderer. Big Bo was certain it was a conspiracy to the crimes connected in Minnesota. He put on his big cowboy hat and grabbed his shotgun out of the police cabinet also he grabbed his favorite gun that he named sawed off Susie.

It was a pump gun that has saved his life numerous of times on the street when he was in shoot outs with drug dealers and thugs. As a precaution he brought along another gun which he named Babe which he placed in the trunk of the patrol car. Big Bo knew there was a connection in the string of crimes and murders in Minnesota. He knew that the only way he could catch these thugs who was hiding in the Low End was to lay low so he didn't get in a rush or want to be seen also he remained calmed. He went to his favorite store in the nearby town and ordered a dark snack of chicken wings and ordered a six pack of beer even though he was a cop.

His mind was in attack mode and he didn't want to talk to nobody until he had nailed the guys who was committing these string of murders, rapes and kidnapping. Big Bo was dedicated to capturing these bad guys so he hid his patrol squad car on the side of the store where he ordered his food and beer. Surely enough, it was three am in the morning when a black van suddenly fit the description of the yelling woman who was running down the streets.

Big Bo didn't panic, He immediately grabbed sawed off Susie to the rescue. He grabbed his gun and kissed it then turned on the lights to the patrol car and rammed the car once he saw the driver fitted the description of the kidnapper, rapist and murderer.

He had his gun in his hand once he jumped out of the police squad car but the driver of the van sped off. Big Bo fired two warning shots at the vehicle and warned them to stop. He also saw Minnesota license plates which was a dead giveaway that there was a connection to the crimes that was occurring in the Low End to the crimes in Minnesota.

The deputy jumped back in his patrol car after the van continued to drive off. Big Bo didn't have back up in the small town so he radioed in ahead for the state trooper but in his mind he knew that he had to apprehend these crooks and bring them to justice himself.

Shots were fired at the only high sheriff on the scene. He got low in the sheriff patrol car. Big Bo manage to raise up and fire a crucial shot through his windshield because the passenger in the black van had shot his whole front windshield out of his sheriff patrol car.

He had in his favorite gun sawed off Susie in his right hand. He fired it again and struck the driver of the black van who immediately wrecked the van. Big Bo was afraid he had injured the women in the van but luckily the women were not in the van they were hidden under a blue tarp in the back lawn of an old abandoned house.

The High Sheriff approached the black van and placed sawed off Susie to the driver's head and warned him one false move and he would kill him dead.

He also warned the passenger he would also be shot if he moved as well. This was not going to be easy when Big Bo fired sawed off Susie, he struck the gas tank on the van and it sprung a leak.

So it was difficult to arrest these thugs while there was a gas leak in the van. The Sheriff was a big man so he pulled both guys through the window. He warned them that he didn't have anything to lose for shooting them if they tried anything.

Finally, he got the handcuffs on these guys and slammed them into his patrol car seat. The State Trooper did finally arrive and told Big Bo, “I see you don’t need any help here.” He replied, “I don’t need no help as long as I got sawed off Susie with me.” “Where are the girls you abducted?” One of the men said, “They are in the abandoned house with a blue tarp around the back of the house.”

The high sheriff of town showed them the barrel of the gun and told them if you are lying to me you will see what my gun sawed off Susie can do!" "I must warn you she is one hell of a dozy if you get her pissed off."

The state Trooper accompanied Big Bo back to the crime scene and sure enough, the daughter of the lady who was running down the streets was found duct tapped. A string of women from Minnesota was also found inside the blue tarp located in the back yard. You could tell these women was not from the south because they had northern accents.

The women praised Big Bo for rescuing her

daughter and the other girls who was from Minnesota and gave old Big Bo a hug. He still had his hand on the trigger on sawed off Susie and he told these criminal, “You don’t stand a chance with me and my gun, I’m Big Bo and you will never see daylight again and if I ever have to chase you again, I promise you that my gun sawed off Susie will lose you!” The town officer known as Big Bo was known to get his man.

His plan was to bring you in alive and if that didn’t work then his plan was just to bring you in. Everyone in the Low End loved Big Bo and he enjoyed doing his job as well. It was a tough job but somebody had to do it, it may seem hard but everyone in a town or community needs someone like Big Bo someone who really loves the people.

Cp. 2 The Car Wash

In the Low End there really wasn't too many opportunities but if you was lucky you were able to land a job at the car wash. The car wash was paying good money for a person in the hood that was serious about working and the name of the car wash was Leroy's car wash.

He wouldn't hire you unless you were 18 years of age. Music was played all day long down at the car wash and people was hustling all day long. Some sold cd, other sold cell phones and tablets. It didn't matter what each individual hustle was at the car wash, Leroy the owner did not care as long as no one disrespected him.

To be honest with you Leroy didn't care even if you sold marijuana on the parking lot but he didn't play selling hard controlled substance drugs at his car wash. If you kept your nose clean and the police didn't get called to the carwash Leroy was fine.

Right next to Leroy car wash was an empty lot, it used to belong to a well-known established African American activist in Philadelphia. The place was a place for change in the community it was called Active Change. Many activists were found at this business seeking change in their culture of life.

Ironically enough the building in the next vacant lot was burned to the ground in a heated debate over change for African Americans rights and the office building became under fire from a riot and was burned to the ground but the empty lot remains right beside Leroy's and served as a place where people shoot dice and beg for money when they see someone pass by. The car wash was the bomb even though it was a car wash it had two long eight hour shifts resulting in sixteen-hours a day. The car wash opened from 0700 am to 12 pm and someone was always available to hand wash your car.

The boss didn't care if the workers smoked weed but he did care how that worker treated himself and the customers. He always told his workers, "It is not what you do, it is how you do it." His moto was no complaint brought to me, no complaint brought to you." You could really earn some good money to take care of your kids working at the car wash. If you were a teen at the age of 18, you could work there and earn enough money to help your parents because times were hard and the economy was extremely rough.

When you give to a community it will come back to you. See even though these people on Mr. Leroy's lot was pan-handling and doing their own thing, they didn't pay Mr. Leroy back. One thing about doing a good deed is, it will come back as payback all on his own.

Even though some of these people who hustled at the car wash was thugs, they had love in their hearts. One night at the car wash things was slow and it wasn't but a few venders or hustlers on the lot. An opportunity was waiting to rob Mr. Leroy and his wife who were at least about eight-five old.

Popo and Betty two known notorious thieves known for stealing, murdering and robbery was hiding in the Low End. People who had high crimes, hid out in the small town for years.

A murderer could go on the run for fifty years in this poor community and no one would ever know anything about it. This neighborhood was never a place for people who thought they were high classed and many people were afraid to live or go near this community.

One night Pobo and Betty these two known notorious crooks tried to rob the elderly millionaire couple at the car wash on the late 12pm midnight shift. They apparently didn't see the drug dealers sitting in the Cadillac on the car wash lot or seemingly they didn't care. It was time for the couple to come out with the money drop for the night which was 10,000 a night this is how much money that was made at the car wash. The 10,000 amount may have not all came from car wash earnings money but it was how to survive in this small town.

Everything may have not been legal but it paid the bills for the community and everything is not everyone else's business either especially when you are trying to survive in a place where no one else is going to give you anything or even come by to check on you.

This project was something like a throw away camp anyway Popo and Betty two known notorious crooks was up very late at night and their plan was to rob the car wash owner Mr. Leroy and his elderly wife but there was one car left on the car wash lot.

The dealers in the Cadillac did in fact see the pair and wondered what were they doing with stocking caps over their face and walking towards the building.

The drug dealers in the car knew right away what was about to take place because they themselves knew the owners schedule.

One of the drug dealers grabbed his gun

and told Betty and Popo that they better leave the parking lot before the ambulance have to come and get them and take them to the hospital for their injuries if they tried to cause any harm to Mr. Leroy or his wife.

The two notorious thieves left immediately before there was harm caused to them. Luckily the car wash owners were safe because they were just about to leave work to go home in two minutes. The guys in the Cadillac warned the couple about what was about to take place but they handled it themselves.

The people on the lot also served as security for the old couple. Just because someone sells drugs doesn't mean in their hearts they are out to hurt someone. I mean, it is wrong to do drugs but every drug dealer is not out to cause harm, some of them are only out to take care of their families.

There were many definition of the Low End, I mean it was mostly definitely a place to live in low extreme conditions especially the low income of many of their residents but the word low End meant a little more too some people living there. The term could have meant that someone has given them the low end of things or someone could have left them out of the good things that were offered in life and handed them the low end of the stick.

There were people walking around like zombies talking to themselves all the time. There were people who were pushing baskets through alleys with all the clothes and everything they owned either on their backs or in the buggy they were pushing.

See the low end could mean the end of a

very low situation. You may never know what a person is going through maybe for you. You can't see it because you never had your kids taken from you or served a long stint prison sentence or tried to recover your life when you got out of prison.

Once you get out of prison, how can you survive then? Some people are strung out on drugs and meth formally known as ice or fentanyl is taking over the street and the minds of the young individual's life. This is a low end literally for them, it is not just a location.

The car wash has made some of the poor kids in the neighborhood famous. Residents sing at the car wash and many artists were made famous because they had incredible voices and if the right recording artist saw them singing, they could be signed to a record label.

They are the ones who gave back to the community. They gave to food banks, churches and whatever it took to keep the building and businesses in the Low End afloat. I mean it takes heart for a person to struggle in a hard low income living environment. Once he or she makes it out the hood and they return to help someone else. This says something about your heart and character.

Some people can make it out of the ghetto or low end places and never return or ever give a dime back to the poor community but they still have their hands out themselves for help. It was always and still is all about them. Many college students paid their way while working at the car wash. There were not many jobs available in Philadelphia, you could work on the trash truck which many people didn't want to do. All of the summer jobs at the school was giving away each year to someone the school knew, it was a buddy- buddy thing at the school.

It was who you knew at the school, it was never based on your merits and your own skills. If your parent knew another parent you were giving a summer job and if no one at the school knew your parents, you were not giving a summer job.

Many people were forced to work in the hot fields on a summer day. The car wash kept everyone safe because everyone looked out for each other. It was all about the hustle and since the people were in the same boat they might as well make this they're own mess together.

You should never look down on anyone in a low situation because you may just never know when it is your time.

People shot dice at the low End car wash and you couldn't judge anyone because people who was supposed to be Christians at the high profile church would sometimes come to the car wash because the car wash was jumping. Celebrities attended the car wash when they came to town. This is how some of the singers who were singing at the car wash was signed to record deal.

Many towns have movie theaters and big town halls to gather in also they have big meetings but in this particular part of Philadelphia, the car wash was entertainment for the residents and it was the best it could get.

You can live your life anyway you want to but you better be very careful when you live your life in the Low End.

Ch. 3 Tyrone fat Burger Joint

Tyrone Fat Burger Joint was located right in the middle of the Low End and it also provided jobs in the poor community.

Everyone loved to go to the burger shack and get a juicy hamburger. They also sold salads too, almost anything you wanted you could find it at the burger shack. It also served as a place where many people met up and saw people who they hadn't saw in years.

Meeting up in the poor town was good and

sometimes it was not so good because sometimes you could meet an old enemy from the past. It was a typical day at Tyrone's burger Joint business was booming as normal when two members of a gang met up on a normal business day and began an altercation in front of the burger joint.

One of the gang members was accused of jumping on the other gang member sister and caused serious injuries to her face and arm. This incident happened years ago but the two guys never saw each other until fifteen years later but each of them had been living in the town.

One gang member called Chico swore he would get the other gang member called Shiloh. The owners called the police to stop the arguing in front of the neighborhood burger shack because everyone was inside enjoying a good delicious hamburger.

Chico, told "Shiloh you better watch your back because you beat up my sister and I'm going to be back for you." Both gang members dispersed and went home.

The business owners and the customers was annoyed by the disruption because some tyrant always wanted to disrupt someone's business and really didn't care about the community. Once Chico got on his cell phone and told his sister Clarissa that he saw Shiloh.

She became hysterical and demanded that her brother do something about it right away.

Suddenly a great order was called into the burger joint, the high school was going on a field trip and decided to stop by old Tyrone's burger joint to see how good his burgers were because everyone worldwide bragged on his famous burgers. Suddenly the school bus pulled into the burger joint and all the high school students were happy. Seemingly trouble was brewing up on the streets and everyone was unaware about this trouble even both gang members because even though Chico threatened Shiloh and promised to get him later, he really wasn't going to do anything he was just bluffing with him.

However, when his sister Clarissa learned that Shiloh was found living in the Low End all these years she demanded he gets hurt and feels the same pain she felt years ago. Chico told his sister, “Shiloh will get what is coming to him someday, there is no need to bring up old trouble.” His sister became furious and said, “My brother won’t even take up for me and will let a creep like Shiloh beat up his own sister.” Chico warned his sister that he loved her but more violence could happened if he confronted Shiloh.

Everything that Chico told his sister fell upon deaf ears at this present time Clarissa had a boyfriend who took the matters very seriously and said he will confront Shiloh when he sees him on the street. The scene was evening on a beautiful lovely day, the sky was blue and the students from the high school was enjoying their lunch at Tyrone's famous burger joint in the Ghetto. Once again Chico was unaware that his sister was seeking revenge on her attacker who broke her arm and hospitalized her years ago. Chico's sister Clarissa manage to gain a large support to help her fight Shiloh.

Trouble was brewing in the community only Chico didn't know anything about it.

Clarissa contacted many of her ladies friends also a few male friends and told them to come out and help her fight. She said the guy who broke her arm and caused her serious bodily harm was last seen in the daytime at Tyrone's burger shack. An angry mob appeared suddenly in front of the burger shack and began to beat on the walls of the building with sticks and many of them had weapons.

Someone threw a flaming bottle cocktail and it managed to start a fire in the burger joint. It had to be evacuated fast because the high school students were still in the burger joint eating food and enjoying themselves. Later there were more people fighting in the streets for no reason at all which made it hard to evacuate the place in order to get the students out to safety.

The flaming bottle cocktail caused black smoke which immediately covered the eyes of almost everyone and filled most of the people lungs with black smoke.

The police were called and they managed to provide an escape way through the nearest alley because the windows was busted out of the school buses and the tires were slashed. No one was injured real badly but now all the students had to be treated at Philadelphia Hospital because of the black smoke they received in their lungs.

No one really knew why the altercation which turned into a brawl began because no one ever saw Shiloh the enemy to begin with. Chico sister had to go back into the hospital to be treated for the same broken arm because she fell on it.

Now she had to explain to her brother why did she go behind his back and get her boyfriend to go start a fight a the fat burger shack which was burned to the ground because of the bottle cocktail that was thrown.

One of the town's leading business was now destroyed and people lost much money. Clarissa had to be hospitalized for a broken arm and smoke inhalation. The streets in the Low End was blocked with yellow streets signs that read, "Police Line Do Not Cross."

The town was now flooded with water

from the old fire trucks that moved very slowly and the sewer was not properly working so the small town was flooded and many people couldn't drive their cars to work and this caused the neighborhood to lose money. The students from the hospital all checked out ok and was released from the hospital in good condition.

The t.v media interviewed Tyrone and he said the cause was because of old beef between two rivals. He also said the loss of his burger joint would affect the poor community for years to come because there were no way he could receive any grant or federal money to rebuild Tyrone's restaurant in a very short time.

The only fat burger joint in town was reduced to ashes and all that was left was a yellow police line that read, "Police line do not cross." Tyrone sustained a broken heart that wouldn't heal anytime soon.

Chp. 4 The Low End Church

The Low End Church was located on the back street on the Low End down the gravel road. Every Sunday and certain nights, special revival services were held at this church.

Now no one can be judged because of their location because people are the same wherever they go. One particular Sunday morning, Sunday school services were being held at the church. Well it was early in the morning so people were glad to see each other some greeted each other with a kiss, hugged, and embraced each other. It was around 12 pm now and some of the members were beginning to get tired of each other as the day went on.

One member of the church asked the other member why they didn't put any money in the offering. Once the deacon asked Sister Jenny this question, she became very offensive and said. "I put my money in the collection plate."

She then shouted out a loud expletive curse word and have to be escorted out of the church by the members. I must say Sister Jenny who was a faithful member was very hot on this

purse screamed out, "Get the purse," "Get the purse." Everybody in the church ran in the business meeting but luckily no one was hurt and sister Patsy was drove home by her son but she was not a happy sister, she fussed all the way home.

Now on a different day a lawn care service guy was hired to cut the grass at the church and it was a hot typical day.

Now keep in mind the church was a poor church located in the Low End so the members had to hire someone very affordable. The guy who cut the grass at the church was someone they knew. It was about 100 degrees in the sun but Jimmy the grass service lawn guy did cut the grass exactly like the members asked him to do. Once Jimmy was finished cutting the grass in the evening time, he came inside of the church to collect his money.

Once he entered the church his eyes were red as a red hot coal but he was very polite when he asked Deacon Sanders for his cash for cutting the grass. Deacon responded to him, “We are having business meeting once we finish I will give you your money." Mr. Jimmy didn't really like the deacon's answer but he said, "Ok I will be back after a while to get my money."

He left the church and headed to town where he had a couple of drinks. Well business in the church continued as the evening passed by the members were standing in the church alter and was about to pray to end the devotion for the day.

While standing in the church alter Mr. Jimmy the lawn care guy came and once again asked deacon Sanders for his money.

Once again deacon told him he was busy right now and didn't have time to give him his cash because he was in a business meeting.

Well finally Mr. Jimmy exploded into an argument near the church alter and said, "You better get me my damn money right now." His fist was balled up like he was ready to hit Deacon Sanders and his eyes were red as if he had been drinking hard liquor.

The two children who was standing near the alter became afraid and ran home and told their mother what happened in the church.

There was a church member about thirty-five years old, he was standing on the church porch. He said, "I respect the church and promised he wouldn't fight in the house of the Lord but he would get across the field and kick some butts." This is putting it nice because he actually said he would tear some a**.

The Church was another place you could showcase your singing talents. Many people did believe in the Lord, like I said earlier it didn't have to happen in the Low End. People are the same way wherever you go. If you wanted to show off your best outfit you could show it off at the church. Some considered the church as a fashion show. Suddenly third Sunday approached and the regular Pastor took a vacation to Italy.

He was replaced with interim pastor Rev. Smith. The Church was thinking about kicking Rev out for some of the sinister things he has done in the past. The only thing kept him in the church the whole time is because some of the users said, “Please don’t judge people for what they have done in the past.” Well one of the thing the secondary pastor was known for was preaching while being intoxicated as smelling like alcohol.

Well third Sunday did arrive and as usual Pastor Smith did show up drunk again as normal. His baby mama dropped him off in a pimped out BMW and he had his fur coat on. Pastor Smith also wore heavy Jewelry around his neck and his beeper went off.

He told his baby mama to page him when she got ready to come back to church. He kissed his baby mama and told her good-bye. The members of the church really began to talk about his behavior in church. Some of the lady members didn't hold back on the pastor, they talked loud enough so he could hear their conversations about not wanting him at this church.

The pastor was known for preaching his best sermons while he was drunk, however even though he was drunk he said he was preaching from his heart but it was not enough for some members. While entering the pulpit to preach for third Sunday service, a pair of dice fell out of his pockets also a joint rolled cigarette felled to the floor. One member picked up this as evidence to hold so they could show it to the main pastor Mr. Tremble who was out on vacation in Italy.

When Rev Smith sermon was over nobody clapped for him on third Sunday. He called his baby momma on the cell phone and said, “Come get me, I am ready to go.” She came to pick him up in the BMW. When Rev Smith left he asked everyone in the church not to judge him and he also said, “He loved everybody.” He waved into the crowd of church members as he departed the church to get in the car with his baby mama. A half full whisky bottle fell from his back pockets and chattered into pieces.

Sister Shelia, one of the ushers of the church said out loud, “This is his last time preaching here at the Low End Church.” “This guy is a disgrace and he has to be voted out of this church.”

“Let’s form a committee and put him out of the church.” Mr. Whitaker was the man who found the rolled joint cigarette and the pair of crooked dice on the floor of the church. Mr. Whitaker said let's put the evidence in a zip lock bag and wait for pastor tremble to come back so we can start a process of voting him out of the church.

The evidence to vote Pastor Smith out of the church was collected and placed into the church vault until the head pastor could come and review these samples.

Sister Jenny could not wait she was the head pastor of the church mistress and had his private cell phone number. She called Pastor

Tremble while he was on his vacation in Italy and began to tell him all the madness that Reverend Smith did in the church third Sunday. Sister Jenny also asked the head pastor was their date still on for next Saturday.

Well see it was certainly not a time to judge Pastor Smith for preaching while he was drunk on third Sunday devotional service because everyone was doing their own sinful thing in the church but they wanted to vote out Mr. Smith. Sister Jenny also told the head pastor of the church, "A rolled joint cigarette fell from his pockets and also a pair of crooked dice." Reverend Tremble as the sister, "How do you know they were a pair of crooked dice?" She said, "Before Mr. Whitaker could seized the pair of dice he noticed the dice looked suspicious."

"He called Brother Alexander in the back room and they began shooting dice." Brother Alexander noticed everyone time he rolled the dice they hit lucky seven every time.

The pastor was astonished, he asked Sister Jenny, "Do you mean to tell me Brother Alexander and Brother Whitaker was shooting dice in the back of the church with a pair of crooked dice?" His Mistress lady said, "Yes they were." The only question the head pastor of the Low End Church said was, "Well who won?" "I remember when Deacon Whitaker in his younger days shot a hell of a dice game and yes we are still on for our hot date this Saturday night Sister Jenny."

See all of these people were trying to remove Pastor Smith out of the church for preaching while he was intoxicated however they were doing their own sinful thing, yet they were trying to remove Rev Smith. The members were throwing a rock and hiding their hands. Even though they drew up plans to have Reverend Smith removed from the church, the head pastor didn't want any parts of removing him because all of them had sinned.

Well the church board held a meeting to remove Pastor Smith from the congregation but when the votes were counted the board was dead locked. 133 members voted to remove Reverend Smith and 133 members voted to keep him at the church. An argument erupted in the business meeting. The rules in the congregation stated that when there is a tie on the church board. The rules are the head pastor will cast the last and final vote. Well Mr. Tremble did cast his final vote in. Finally the ruling was read aloud to the church and the rulings were not to remove the backup Pastor from The Low End Church.

When the votes results came in Sister Jenny, the head Pastor church mistress told the pastor, “You damn fool our date is off for Saturday night.” Once the head pastor wife

Mrs. Outlaw heard this. She said, "You been secretly slipping around with my husband." "What was done in the dark has finally came to the light." There were a slight scuffle in the church between the head pastor, his wife and sister Jenny." Sister Jenny wig managed to get pulled off in the struggle and she had a bald head. She picked up her wig off the floor and went home.

The head pastor wife told her, "I ought to get me something in my hands and come see about you sister." "I ought to lay my hands on you and not be praying for you sister. “It was unknown who threw the rock through the church window it happened during the scuffle somehow. There were severe damage caused in the church due to the scuffling in the church. There had to be plans to remove the head pastor from the church for having a mistress in the church.

The deacon called an emergency meeting to have the repairs and damage fixed on the church and also remove the head pastor from the church. It was an emergency overnight decisions which was a unanimous decision to remove the head pastor from the church. Mr. Tremble was removed from the church but what the members didn't realize that now that he was removed from the church the head pastor now would be Mr. Smith the third Sunday Pastor.

Pastor Smith showed up every Sunday morning except for third Sunday with his baby mama. She dropped him off in the pimped out BMW and the members of the Low End Church learned to get alone with him and apologized to him for trying to remove him as interim pastor of the church because suddenly they realized that everyone in the church had sined.

Ch. 5. The Barber Shop

The Low End Barbershop was a place where everyone discussed everybody business in the town. The barber was a great barber also he rented out booths to other barbers who wanted to make a great income. One particular day in the barber shop a guy named switch blade Jimmy came into the barber shop to get his hair cut.

The head barber refused to cut his hair because Switch Blade Jimmy acted a fool earlier the week. He told the head barber man, "I was strung out on them drugs." The barber whose name was Henry asked Switch Blade, "How do you think you are not strung out of them today?" He further ask him how much money do you have. Switch Blade said, "Man I got money, I got enough money to buy your damn shop and send you home broke."

The owner said, "That's enough get out of here at once." Switchblade was slightly sober but still under the effects of hard drugs and alcohol. Well he didn't go by the name of Switchblade Jimmy for nothing. He immediately pulled out a switchblade on the barber. A customer who was waiting to get his hair cut hit Switchblade from the blindside and knocked the razor out of his hand and more of his valued customers of 30 years wrestled him out of the barbershop.

The head barber didn't want to hurt him after all he knew he was on drugs. Once the rudely customer was thrown out, the barber came out of the shop and told him to get his life together. He was lying on the ground and asked Henry the head barber for ten dollars so he could get some food to eat. Henry told him, “I will go next door and get you a plate of food.” Switchblade actually wanted the money for a hit but he didn’t refuse the plate of food because he was hungry he hadn’t ate in two days.

When Henry the barber walked over to the next door to the food store. The owner said, “We value you your patronage Henry but Switch Blade Jimmy is not welcome in Leroy’s New Barbecue joint Henry said, “Well I will pay for the food now and will you bring it outside to give it to him.” “Yes sure, we all try to help

Switchblade but just last week he got high and burst all the windows out of my new burger Joint, and I just rebuilt it after the fire.'' "This is why I have my windows boarded up now."

"Oh, he was the one who broke out your windows?" "Yes he was." "I will have a talk with him about that. "I see he listens to you a lot Henry." "Well he just tried to pull a switchblade out on me just a few minutes.

"He tried to pull a switchblade out of you just minutes ago and you are buying him some food." "Well he didn't cut me my customers threw him out of the barber shop." "Well I guess you are just doing the will of God, I can't blame you for that." Leroy opened the door and said to the drug attic, "Here are your barbecue ribs and potato salad." "You should really think Henry here because I didn't want to serve you."

Henry walked back to the shop after all he had the booth rented so he didn't lose too much money. He advised Switch Blade Jimmy that if he went to drug rehab and become clean he would give him a job in his very own shop. Switch blade real name was Devararis and ironically enough he had a job cutting hair in the barbershop across the streets called New Face Barber Shop. Well Blade told the owner. “I will think about it.” Henry returned to the barbershop and said, “Next in line.”

The customers were happy to get a nice haircut from their favorite barbershop and receive a fresh cut hair and a nice hairline. This wasn’t an all-black barber shop, Henry could cut all types of hair because he learned it in barber training. The next guy was seated in the chair his name was T- money and he was most definitely the town's ladies' man. He drove a Mercedes Benz and worked and earned a high salary. T-money had a mouth full of gold and a hand full of rings and he loved to smile. He just loved women but he was a cool guy that wouldn't hurt anyone. He began to talk about a young lady he went out went.

T-money didn't know that the girl he was speaking about, her boy-friend's brother was seated next to him. He began to tell Henry the barber, "He went out on a date with Lashawndra and she got pregnant but she was with another dude." He also told Henry that the baby was his because her guy was out of town driving trucks." He said, "Man I can't claim no more babies because child support is already on him for the ten kids he got."

The barber looked at him and said, "Brother you are sure right because I see that baby all the time because the mother comes next door to visit Leroy's New Burger Joint."

The whole barbershop notice that the customer who was next in line for a haircut left in a hurry and did not get his haircut. The customer who left in a hurry name was Coolio. He was the brother of the child in question the barber and T-Money was talking about. Once he saw his brother he said, "Lashawndra is playing games with you bro."

"Well what are you saying?" His brother Emanuel said. "Do you know a guy name T-money who drives a BMW?" Emanuel answered him, "He is the only one driving a BMW in the Low End, and I have seen him around of course." "How is Lashawndra playing me brother?" His brother replied to him, "I hate to be the one to tell you this T-money was at barber shop earlier bragging about how the child is not yours." Well Emanuel replied, "I have heard rumors that little Elizabeth was not my child, this is not the first time I have heard this."

Emanuel immediately jumped into his work truck and went to confront T-money about running his mouth. He grabbed some heavy artillery and went to the barbershop in the Low End.

Since they were gossiping a lot in the barbershop, T-money was finished getting his hair cut but he remained in the shop and continue to run his mouth. Once Emanuel entered the grounds of the barbershop, he immediately grabbed his pump gun and went inside to confront T-Money who was still laughing and running his mouth.

The only thing that slowed Emanuel from confronting T-Money was his truck was not in gear and was rolling down the hill because he jumped out in a rush. Switch Blade Jimmy was still outside begging for money and didn't have a clue why Emmanuel jumped out his car in a rush so he yelled quickly, “Your truck is heading down the hill towards the ditch.” This distracted Emanuel because now he has to get his truck from the ditch. He hid the shotgun in his clothing so when Switchblade saw the shotgun, He asked, “What is going happening and why do you have the gun?”

He told Switchblade that he had better mind his business before he send him straight to hell because that is where he is going anyway. The distraction was enough for T-money to leave the barbershop after all Emanuel was planning to shoot T-money and run but he had to chill now because he couldn't get away with it, besides his truck was in the ditch. Even though Emanuel couldn't draw attention to himself now his truck was stranded.

T-money was leaving the barbershop now and proceeded to put his key in the ignition, he was shown the barrel of a gun and told him what would happen if he tried to raise his child or if he keeps running his mouth about the baby in question.

T-Money was shaking with terror he could hardly get the key in the ignition and he reassured Emanuel that he wouldn't have any more problems out of him. Once the barbershop found out what had occurred. They realized that if Switchblade-Jimmy wouldn't have distracted the mad angry man he would have entered the shop with the shotgun and had his way and innocent people would have gotten hurt because the shop was full of people.

This tragic incident allowed Switchblade to be invited back into the barbershop or at least until he started acting crazy on drugs again. The customers were waiting for switchblade to slip but his behavior became normal. Every day he came into the barbershop and ran errands for Henry the owner.

He even emptied the garbage, mopped and swept the floor but most of all he watched Henry cut the customers hair. He already knew how to cut hair and often told Henry, "You are going to high with that hair line on that customer." Henry agreed he was too high with the line and corrected it. Time went by at the

Low End Barbershop.

The more time Switch blade entered the shop and was giving detail duties, the more he became appreciated and being accepted in the community allowed him to change his drugs patterns. Everyone suddenly realized that Devarasis wasn't acting so crazy now and all he does is drink coffee all day.

He found the love of the people and he also found the love of a passion and a craft that he loved, which was cutting hair.

Once Henry the barber saw he was sober

he retrained him to cut hair all over again but his barber license had to be recertified. There was no way Henry would put money into Switchblade hands so he paid for the barber training course himself.

Which wasn't hard because the drug attic cut hair in the past. Once the seven week barber course was over by then Switch Blade was completely sober. He received his barber-training license and became the top man in the barbershop to cut hair ever.

He became so great now that the head

barber Henry would take off days. He saw a change in his co-worker and friend's behavior. Although, he warned him that if he ever screw up things he would go back to the streets and live the life of a modern bum he once lived.

There was no need to tell his worker that because he was tired of sleeping on the grounds and begging for money. Switchblade Jimmy was a changed man and when the customers enters the shop, they love to get their special hair cut by him the new barber. Will all the rumors ever stop in the barbershop? I don't know if they ever will because this is where rumors develop.

Ch. 6 The Soup Line

One of the many advantages about the poor living conditions in the Low End, is there were many residents and churches of the small community would see the struggling small community and do a good deed for the citizens of poverty.

Many organizations contributed food and money to distribute food also the community sponsored cooked meals every day in the community down at the place called Break Bread Center. One day while waiting in a long line to eat food at the Break Bread Center sponsored by the rich Catholics who always played an important role in finding housing for poor residents. It was a long soup line formed in the Low End when one guy named Fisher decided to sell cigarettes two for a dollar.

His hustle was going fine until another person started selling cigarettes for the same price. This caused a verbal altercation in the line. Fisher claimed Sonny was stepping on his toes because he was trying to sell cigarettes and he already knew Fisher began his hustle first.

Fisher told Sonny to step back and Sonny said, "I don't want no trouble man I will stand down."

What he said and what he did was two different things, he continued to sell cigarettes in the soup line.

The soup line was very long but it was moving very fast. It was the only meal that some of them would get for three days. Most of the residents were seated at the Break Bread Center when Fisher began to get loud with Sonny. He walked over to Sonny and broke his whole pack of cigarettes. He took all of his cigarettes and crumbled them up. Then he took all of his information such as social security card and state id from him. Sonny was an ex drug attic who was still struggling with drugs. He also walked with a limp because a car hit him and ran several years ago.

The Catholics warned them both to leave the Break Bread Center at once before we call the police. The people who were eating at the Break Bread Center noticed that Fisher was bullying the smaller crippled person. Many of the people who were eating in this soup line wanted to fight fisher but they knew the rule was in place at the Low End. This rule was even though a person may not have two dollars to their name, it is possible that they had a gun in their possession.

Nearly everyone had a gun even if he was a drug attic and couldn't afford nothing else, he had a gun. The gun was visible that was located on Fisher's waist. The faculty of the Break Bread Homeless Center threw the two people out of their facility for misconducting themselves and violating their rules. Fisher was using expletives words and he vowed he would pay the smaller, crippled person back the next day at the Cemetery. Now the Cemetery was not an actual cemetery, it was another church called Cathedral. It funded food for the homeless people in the hood. The Cathedral opened up early in the morning at eight am because the homeless shelter would not house the residents all day.

It was a cold morning although it was summer, a cold front came through the small poor flats. This church got its name Cemetery because there was many fights at this church. It served meals three times a day but it had a record history of drive by shootings and frequent fights that occurred often. Even the staff was involved in hurting people who came to this church for food and services.

The sad part about it was fighting in this Church was considered normal and no one called the police. If you were injured the staff would drag you outside into the streets and told you not to come back. Homeless did not have a special person to pick, there were many people who were homeless. Little babies was homeless in the summer and they trembled in their baby carriage in the wintertime. Little babies were not exempt from cold weather or rainy weather everyone was homeless. The long line began to proceed inside of the Cemetery Church at eight am in the morning.

While everyone was in the church. Fisher spotted the smaller guy Sonny and walked up to him. He said, “I told you that I would get you if you came to the Cemetery.” Sonny told him, “We have already gotten thrown out of one place and I didn't want to fight or argue with you anymore." Without warning, Fisher began to pistol whip the smaller crippled fellow. Sonny fell to the ground and covered himself up. He managed to stand up on his feet and began to fight because it was the street code.

Even though he was the smallest one, it was mandatory that you still fought because everyone was looking. If you didn't put up a fight other bullies will continue to pick on you. Even though Sonny had heart, there was no way he could beat Fisher in fight. The Low End Code was to step up and help the smaller victim who was in trouble or losing the fight. Big Groceries entered the Cemetery and saw what was taking place. Everyone was scared of him because he had just did a ten-year prison sentence for murder.

Everyone in the cemetery knew that Big Groceries was fresh out of the Penitentiary. Some people referred to him as Big G.

It was a name given to him in the penitentiary meaning that he had a lot of food to eat. He had a lot of money put on his books in the prison. Big Groceries was fresh out of the penitentiary. He was a big solid guy. He grabbed the bully and put him in a choke hold. He also put a gun to his head. Then all of a sudden, Big G. became nervous and started shaking.

The last time he started shaking was when he lost controlled and killed a man over ten cents he lost in a crap game. Fisher was surprised, he didn't know the rules of The Low End was to help the man in trouble or losing the battle.

It was the projects code and Big Groceries

told the bully, “If he ever bothered Sonny again they would find him a nearby alley somewhere stinking.” “I just did ten years in prison and I will do twenty more standing on my head for a chump like you.” When Big Groceries turned the bully lose, frantically he began to run. Nobody ever heard from him again.

Fisher was so afraid for his life, he called his sister who was an evangelist and informed her that his life was in trouble. She sent him a bus ticket, he caught a bus ride to Mississippi and no one ever heard or saw him again. Big G told

Sonny that, “He admired him for fighting the bully even though it seemed like he couldn’t win.” Good news was about to happen for Sonny because the Catholics approved his housing brochure and found him a place to live and he didn’t have to live on the streets anymore around people who were bullies.

Sonny decided he would return the favor for Big Groceries for helping him stand up to the bully. He was smart with computer skills so he helped Big G completed his housing application also he allowed him to live with him until he got situated. The people living in the low-end situations may not have had money but they had each other. Money isn't everything and it cannot buy happiness only love and sticking up for each other brings happiness. One thing the people in the Low End learned is, only doing the will of God will stand.

Sticking together was necessary because residents didn't have any money. Many of them was receiving government assistance such as government cell phones and food stamps. Love didn't cost a thing and helping others don't cost a thing. Many people get infatuated with material things and get inequity in their heads, which sometimes causes them to think they are more than the next person is. When you leave this world, you are not going to take anything with you! No matter how rich you are. Seemingly, you are not going to take any of your money with you. You are going to stand before God and be judged by your works and you had better pray that your name is written in the book of life.

Ch. 7. The Welfare Office

A welfare office was located in the middle of the poor housing complex. This office served as a place for poor residents to get established for food stamps Medicaid and other supplement that a poor person needed.

A guy named Humphrey who was not in his right state of mind took a number and stood in the welfare line. Security told him, "To put his shoes on and pull his pants up." Humphrey didn't have a belt in his pants nor did he have strings in his shoes and he did not have any of the information he needed to qualify for benefits at the welfare office. He sat his beer can down on the outside of the welfare office for later. The security officers warned him not to cause any trouble. The receptionist finally called his number to get assistance.

The nice woman asked him, "What can we do for you today?" It turned out that he was smarter than everyone thought." He went into his pants and got a note and passed it to the clerk window. The note said, "Give me all your money and don't say a word or move." The clerk wondered did he have a gun because he had to entered the security clearance. It was the welfare protocol to follow procedures in their manual for robberies.

Since it was a welfare office, there was not very much money in the drawer. The clerk did exactly what the robber asked her to do. She gave him all the money that was left in the drawer for the whole day. The amount was $17.50 cents. Humphrey became angry, this alerted security that something was wrong in the booth window. Still the window clerk had to follow protocol and give him all the money if she wanted to keep her job. She told him the welfare was a place that help people with resources and this was all the money earned for the whole day.

Anyway the operator handed the money to him and he tried to walk calmly out of the office when security was alerted of the robbery in place. He ran out of the welfare office and grabbed his beer he left outside and began to run into the Low End Community. The guards were trained well and were informed never to shoot while the children and staff was inside of the building because someone innocent could get shot. He made off with the $17.50 at least for now. There was a crap game going on in the parking lot of the welfare office.

A robbery was normal in this place so people saw him running down the street and proceeded with their normal routine. Big Bo was still the town's Sheriff everyone relied on. He was called by dispatch to bring Humphrey in for his robbery of $17.50. The High Sheriff went to the nearest drug house in the hood and kicked the door down. He found Humphrey sniffing on a powered substance. He immediately arrested him on the spot at once. The suspect was taken into the County jail and was awaiting court trial.

He stood trial without a paid lawyer but he was appointed a court lawyer. Humphrey told the judge and jury that, "He wasn't planning to rob the welfare office." "He was there to get assistance when the clerk got the message confused and handed him $17.50 cents." "He took the money and bought him a hit of drugs." Finally, the judge asked him, "If you didn't demand the money then why did you accept or spend the money?" Humphrey told the lady judge, "This is my business and not yours so stay out of my business lady."

The judge became hysterical and threw the gavel at him but she knew she didn't have a case against him. There was no place to put him because of Covid the jails were crowded. Even though he robbed the welfare office, it could not be proven because he did not have a gun in his possession. Another reason the charges didn't stick was in the state of Philadelphia, $17.50 was considered a petty crime. The judge told Humphrey, "He was a low-classed disgrace to society and one day he will get what is coming to him." She also told him, "He needed to go take a bath at once because the whole court room is funky because of you." He was released back to the streets at once.

The people in the Low End could not believe he was able to come back to the projects. He went back into the welfare office the very next day and tried to do the exact same thing. Drugs played an important role in this community.

The Low End was a community where anything goes and this community governed itself. It was set apart from the rest of the real world and the people there had no clue what real life consisted of.

Humphrey did not care or even knew what he did. Big Bo the community Sherriff saw him and did a double take. He told Humphrey, “The law may not get you and take you into custody but don’t you let the smooth taste fool you.” “I will get my man one way or the other.” “The next crime you commit in this town, I will fix it where nobody else will ever see you again." He banged his head against the police car and told Humphrey, "See there is no law in this place and my word is law so don't mess with me boy." He placed his pump gun Sawed off Susie to his head and placed his hands on the trigger. "I got murderers and thugs out here to deal with."

"I got to stop helping people to come deal with your sorry low classed butt." "I promise you next time it won't be too pretty for you either." He fired his favorite gun Sawed off Susie in the air around a crowd of people even little children. He slapped Humphrey in the face with the barrel of the gun, it sounded out very loud then he drove off in the squad car. The small poor community needed Sheriff Big Bo because like he said there was no law in the place. Big Bo made the laws and no one ever confronted him about the choices he made in this projects.

The next time Humphrey was seen in the Low End he was clean and sober. I heard he was passing out church pamphlets and working hard for the church. He was a changed man, he saved his social security money and found him a wife. He told the Big Bo the only Sheriff in town that he saved his life when he was going down the wrong pathway and he will never make that mistake again. Night fell in the community and people walked around all night long as if it was still daylight. The poor community never slept, you could get anything you wanted from dust to dawn.

The town didn't have laws but it governed itself. You can live by your own laws or you could die by your own laws and even though there were no laws in place, you could make or break yourself with your own thinking.

Big Bo was in his Patrol car located nearly five minutes from the poor community. He was on duty drinking a six pack of beer and eating chicken wings. He wasn't given a special crime dog so he used his own dog which was a Pitt Bull he used to intimidate folks after all, who was going to say anything to the only town's Sheriff Big Bo.

Ch. 8 Government Cheese Line

It was a beautiful day in the hood and everyone were lined up at the social security office building to receive a block of government cheese. Everyone in the low-income community was entitled to receive a package of honey, pork powder eggs and a block of government cheese.

A family could benefit from certain programs if their income was very low. Many of the residents in this small community didn't have a father in the house available. Some of the family members only had mothers to help pay the bills and the children were very small and could not help until they became old enough. One typical day the family were lined up in the Low End Community to receive their commodity package.

Everything was going fine until someone jumped in the cheese line. It was a small scuffle at the social security office because Mrs. Johnson accidentally forgot her spot in the line and got in front of the wrong participant. Mrs. Johnson was about seventy-years old and could not see very well. She went to her car for a minute and when she came back, she accidentally got in front of Mrs. Alexander. Mrs. Alexander shouted out a racist slur, which said, “Black folks don’t know how to act.” She further added, “White folks don’t act like this.” Well there were nearly all races in line.

Her speech did not go along well with the other African Americans that were in the government cheese line. “How dare you talk about black people in front of all these people,” said Mrs. People. Mrs. Johnson grandson was in the car still, he heard the commotion and came to defend his Grandmother. "He pulled a blade and said, "I just got out of juvenile and I will go back if someone tries to hit my grandmother over a block of damn Government cheese." "We shouldn't have to live this way, we should be helping each other out."

"Don't never put my race down in front of no other race, hell Africans Americans built this country and we didn't receive a quarter." He said with a deep heavy voice. It was a political and race war outside of the cheese line. The staff inside the building heard the loud noise and ran out to see what was happening. The head staff in charged told all the cheese recipients that if they continued to be rude outside they would go home without a cheese package. This really made things worst in the poor community.

One African American male told another African American guy to his face, “See what you did now N?” “Don’t you call me no N word because you are blacker than I am,” said the other African American. “If I go home without getting my cheese box I’m going to pull out my box razor," said a lady who appeared to be white." "I thought you said white people don't act like that in public," Said Jimmy."

"Only a few whites act rude in public and black people always show out no matter where they go," said Ester. "You better stop talking about my ancestors," said another woman. The staff saw this turmoil outside and opened the door.

They began to distribute the cheese packages in order to break the fight up. Many of the residents who were still in line received their cheese commodity package. Others who were fighting outside did not receive theirs. Some of the citizens were down in the ditch fighting. Seemingly fighting is worth more than getting their commodity cheese package.

The law was called for the people who was fighting. Big Bo the Sheriff was on vacation, he only took one-day vacation so that he wouldn't miss out on any activity in the town.

The town's fire department was activated to assist this matter. The dispatcher said, "Do we need more back up units." The acting Sheriff and another district precinct answered, "No we got enough units to clean up this mess." Another Precinct was activated to assist in this brawl fight. Everyone fighting was placed in the patty wagon were taken to the Low End jail, where the rats are starving in the cells.

These rats are so hungry that they eat on the prisoners who are brought to the jail. One African American woman named Mrs. Love told the people who was fighting, "Yawl going to hell for fighting and the people are trying to bless us." She further continue to say, "This is why black people can't have nothing. She actually she said the expletive word that starts with a S. "Black folks can't do nothing right, then they get mad when the white folks talks about us."

"There is not one Mexican out here fighting because they learn to get alone." "Let me get my cheese box and go home and cook me some nice cheese sandwiches." "Take their butts to jail Captain," she said. The jails were crowded in the Low End but Big Bo was off work and could not maintain the disorderly bunch. Some of the Africans American spray-painted "Black Power" on the side of the social security office. Big Bo the town's Sheriff always watched the news at home because he never slept.

He sent a message to the police department that said, "I will clean things up in the morning when I get on duty." This fighting in the cheese line made the evening news. The headline read. "Big fight in cheese line in the Low End, few hospitalized." It also made the Sun Times Newspaper, it was captioned, "Big fight in the Government cheese line in the Low End, few injured and jailed." A spokesperson for the

Negro league issued a statement to the brothers and sisters of the Low End community to hold your heads up. “We must fight with dignity and strength, we must never lose our unity as a whole.” News center 11 got the word late about the fight in the cheese line. They arrived on the scene to record a broadcast for their evening news. When they arrived, there were only one Hispanic woman that couldn’t Speak English very fluent still standing at the scene.

Channel 11 News Center asked her what happened. She said, “Black folks got to fighting and some went to jail." The next day Sheriff Big Bo returned to duty early so he could see the people who were jailed while he was off duty. He was surprised to see his Grandmother in jail for fighting in the government cheese line.

He said, "Let my grandmother out of the cell at once." "Where is your glasses and your wig Grandmother?" She answered, "Baby, I lost my wig and glasses in the scuffle at the social security office."

"I didn't even get my cheese either those bastards." Well there was nothing for the High

Sheriff to say now. Everyone in the fight was given time served and allowed to go home. Well since the Sheriff Grandmother was involved in the fight, the only thing Big Bo could do was wait in the Sheriff patrol car with his mouth closed.

Some people walked around in the streets holding up signs that reads, "No Justice No peace." It was their constitutional rights but the best method of demonstration is to never lose your head. Some things are not worth fighting for. It could take you a lifetime to achieve your goals but it could take you only seconds to lose everything you ever owned in life. I have one rule that I apply. A fisherman can fish all day long but if the fish don't ever bite the hook, he wouldn't ever catch a fish. We have to decipher and identify the problem without fighting the issue and causing a real bigger problem.

See it was important for the residents to receive the food but it was not important to cause a brawl because many of them received jail time and also a hospital bill. Why did they receive this type of treatment? It is because they didn't think the problem out in its entirety.

When we plan, we must also think as well. It does not do us any good if we put the wagon in front of the mule. We defeat our purpose when we lose our head. The most weapon we could ever lose is our minds. It don't make no different if you are white, black, Hispanic rich or poor.

The most effective tool you can use is your mind. A poor man can become a rich man if he uses his mind. If he doesn't become a rich man, he will always be considered wealthy in knowledge. As long as God allows the winds to keep blowing a poor man could always become a wealthy or a rich man but if he loses his mind, this is the point where he loses everything. We as people have to know when we lose the game.

There is no sense in losing and continue on trying to win, when the game was lost a long time ago. We as a whole has to figure out at what point we lost what we was fighting for.

Once we analyze the point where we went wrong, we should use corrective measures to correct the problem right away and not proceed further into destruction. What I am saying is the people who went to the social security office for food found it necessary to fight in the streets. They found it necessary to fight for the rights and equality at a pivotal and critical time.

The people needed what was immediate to them and the cheese commodity was pivotal to them. Food was more important but they started fighting for rights and equality and they were already free. We can lose anything in life but it is critical that we do not lose our heads or minds. We can hold up injustice signs all day long but we when lose our own heads, the blame is all on us. It is imperative as a nation also as a whole that we remain and stay focused. No man or woman is in poverty as long as the Lord is with them. No man is down and out no matter how low the community is. It don't matter if society has written you off. It doesn't matter if you were given the low end of the deal.

You have to consider if you have one fight left inside of you and if you do, I suggest you use it wisely.

There is no such thing as one race being better than the next race especially when you are all in the same boat and in this case, they were all poor people. Only you can lose you, only you can defeat you and this only happens when you give up or quit.

Ch. 9. Christmas Fell In The Low End

You could tell what time of the year it was in the Low End. Decorations were placed all over the town. Even the fire trucks had Christmas ornaments on them. You could hear the sounds of Christmas music in the air. There were a celebration at the only church in town. Pastor Smith who became the church preacher after the main pastor was voted out of the church. This is why he was still preaching at the Low End Church. Many members tried to vote him out as third Sunday interim pastor because he would always come to the church drunk. Well the members was unsuccessful to vote him out of the church because they had sins that were hidden themselves.

The church presented a Christmas play for the community to watch. There were mostly children who participated in the church. Rev Smith drinking had gotten worst. While the play was going on Rev. reached into his pockets and took a swig of hard bourbon whiskey, he put the remaining liquor back into his pockets. His baby momma was First Lady of the church now. The

BMW they drove to church was parked outside. He was not completely drunk, he was always intoxicated and he delivered some of his best sermons while he was drunk.

The play was well orchestrated and presented just fine. There were still loud whispers of not wanting Rev. Smith as the church pastor. When his baby momma who was sitting next to him finally woke him up a blunt cigar was rolled, it felled on the floor. His baby momma was dressed up very nice. She wore make-up and fine jewelry. She is the reason why he remained in the church for a long period. She always looked after the pastor. I mean she was much younger than he was but she was actually the one who kept him in line.

Alberta was her name, she smoked marijuana but she did not drink. The church did admire his baby momma, they just didn't like the pastor sinful ways. When the play was over it was time to eat and present the gifts.

The ushers were ready to serve the food and present the gifts when they noticed the gifts were gone. Only one person had departed the church and he was long gone by now. He was a known thief who stole all the gifts while everyone had their heads down praying. It was notorious crook Lil Johnny. No one detected him leaving the church with the Christmas toys.

Well, all the members could do now was serve the food because the kids now didn't have any toys and they were very sad. "Deacon Sanders said, "This is a very long gravel road to walk on and the thief couldn't have gotten very far." "We can ride down on him and make him surrender the gifts." "I got something in my pockets that will make him drop it like it's hot. "No Deacon Sanders, don't get yourself in trouble because the thief will get what is coming to him." "I don't like nobody who makes kids sad," said Deacon Sanders.

Well the first lady of the church said, "We have been robbed today but we still have to give thanks and not forget the true meaning of Christmas." "It is not just presents, we are here to give thanks to our savior that was born today." Meanwhile on the outstretch of town the town's Sheriff was playing Santa Claus at the town hall. He was presented with the High Sheriff Awards. On his way to the assembly, he was happy and singing joyful chorus.

Ole Big Bo the town's Sheriff has been through some hard shifts but he was happy to fight crime in the Low End. The Santa Claus suit he had on was too tight and he couldn't button up the last button.

He wasn't scheduled for his honored Sheriff event until about two hours later. He wanted to get a little drink before he went to the town hall to receive the Sheriff award. He was sitting in his car when all of a sudden, he noticed a male figure coming down the gravel road with a large sack on his back.

Big Bo didn't know Lil Johnny had robbed the children's gifts from the church. However he knew something was wrong because he had arrested the thief numerous of times. There was nothing the Sheriff could do without proof after all people steal all the time in the Low End.

He waved at the thief but Lil Johnny gave it all away when he began to run. Big Bo told him, "Stop or I will blow a damn whole in you on

Christmas day you bum." "Where did all these gifts come from?" "I don't know said Johnny."

"Since you ran from me, it is probable cause to take you in to jail on Christmas." "Please don't take me to jail on Christmas," said Johnny." "Son don't play with me, look down the barrel of this gun," said the angry Sheriff. "I will blow a hole in you bigger than a mayonnaise jar if you don't tell me where you stole these gifts from."

"I will tell you just don't take me to jail sir." "I stole the gifts from the church." "What you bastard," said Big Bo. "Get in this Sheriff car right now I'm taking you to jail for Christmas." "You said you wouldn't take me to jail today Sir." "I didn't tell you anything like that boy."

"You are going to jail today for stealing from the church." "You get out of my patrol squad car you piece of junk." "I will catch you stealing later for sure because you are a regular. Thief."

He was a busy Sheriff, he had a man of honor award ceremony in just about thirty minutes to attend. He had to hurry to the church to give the gifts back to the children. Once he arrived at the church with the bag of gifts the mood began to change everyone was happy.

The members said, “It was awful nice of you to bring these gifts to these poor children. A thief who we invited into our own church stole the gifts we had bought the children’s and some of the gifts were our gifts.

The officer told them, “It was Lil Johnny who stole the gifts from this church and I am just returning them to everyone.” “I can’t stay because I got a man of honor award ceremony to attend in ten minutes." The little kids eyes began to light up for Christmas and the Pastor said, "This cause for a drink and turned up his whiskey bottle.

This time he fell by the Christmas tree but his baby momma had his back. "She told the little kids and some deacons to help her put him in the BMW." She drove him home later, the pastor was lucky to have a baby momma like Alberta. She had respect and respect went a long ways in the church. Once everyone ate and received their gifts, they departed the church.

All except for Rev Smith who was drunk in the car. Once everyone left the parking lot she fired up her blunt and usher Jenny said, “Let me hit that blunt sister girl.” “For sure,” said the first lady. It was a fantastic Christmas time in the Low End after all, for all.

Made in the USA
Monee, IL
24 August 2023